Dear Parent:
Your child's love of reading starts here!

Every child learns to read in a different way and at his or her own speed. Some go back and forth between reading levels and read favorite books again and again. Others read through each level in order. You can help your young reader improve and become more confident by encouraging his or her own interests and abilities. From books your child reads with you to the first books he or she reads alone, there are I Can Read Books for every stage of reading:

SHARED READING
Basic language, word repetition, and whimsical illustrations, ideal for sharing with your emergent reader

BEGINNING READING
Short sentences, familiar words, and simple concepts for children eager to read on their own

READING WITH HELP
Engaging stories, longer sentences, and language play for developing readers

READING ALONE
Complex plots, challenging vocabulary, and high-interest topics for the independent reader

I Can Read Books have introduced children to the joy of reading since 1957. Featuring award-winning authors and illustrators and a fabulous cast of beloved characters, I Can Read Books set the standard for beginning readers.

A lifetime of discovery begins with the magical words **"I Can Read!"**

Visit www.icanread.com for information
on enriching your child's reading experience.

I Can Read® and I Can Read Book® are trademarks of HarperCollins Publishers.

Pete the Cat's Trip to the Supermarket
Copyright © 2019 by James Dean
Pete the Cat is a registered trademark of Pete the Cat, LLC.
All rights reserved. Manufactured in U.S.A.
No part of this book may be used or reproduced in any manner whatsoever without written permission except
in the case of brief quotations embodied in critical articles and reviews. For information address HarperCollins
Children's Books, a division of HarperCollins Publishers, 195 Broadway, New York, NY 10007.
www.icanread.com

Library of Congress Control Number: 2018952744
ISBN 978-0-06-267538-5 (trade bdg.) — ISBN 978-0-06-267537-8 (pbk.)

19 20 21 22 23 LSCC 10 9 8 7 6 5 4 3 2
Book design by Jeanne Hogle
❖
First Edition

I Can Read!

BEGINNING READING 1

Pete the Cat's
TRIP TO THE SUPERMARKET

by Kimberly &
James Dean

HARPER

An Imprint of HarperCollinsPublishers

Pete and Bob are hungry
after a big day of fun
at the park.

"Dad, can we have a snack?"

Bob asks.

Dad checks
the fridge.

Dad checks
the pantry.

Dad checks
the secret snack nook.

6

"We need to buy groceries,"
says Dad.

Dad starts to make a list.
"We need milk and eggs
and fish and chicken."

"I want raspberries," says Bob.

"I want apples," says Pete.

Pete, Bob, and Dad

make a long list

and take it to the supermarket.

Oh no!

The wind blows the list

out of Dad's hands.

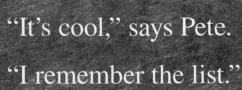

"It's cool," says Pete.

"I remember the list."

"I do too," says Bob.

First they stop in aisle ten.

The sign says Dairy.

"We need milk," says Pete.

"And cheese," says Bob.

"The stinky kind."

Next they go to aisle nine.

"Yum," says Dad.

"I love bacon!"

"Don't forget the chicken,"

says Pete.

They almost pass aisle eight

when Pete remembers eggs.

"Regular or jumbo?" asks Pete.

"Jumbo," says Dad.

"Groovy," says Pete.

Bob can't pick between
spaghetti and macaroni
in aisle seven.

"How about bow ties?"

asks Dad.

"Awesome," says Bob.

Aisle six smells fruity.

"Remember the apples," says Pete.

"Remember the raspberries," says Bob.

In aisle five

Dad tastes a hot dog.

Yummy!

In aisle four

Pete tastes a cupcake.

Sweet!

Dad lets Pete and Bob

choose a treat in aisle three.

26

Pete picks crackers

shaped like fish.

Bob picks popcorn.

Brrr! It's cold in aisle two.

Dad puts mango popsicles

in the cart.

29

Aisle one has

sunflowers, tulips,

and blue daisies.

Pete and Bob pick tulips

for Grandma.

"She'll love them," says Dad.

"I think we got everything

except the fish!" says Dad.

But their car is packed

with yummy treats.

Next time!